Andi's Fair Surprise

Circle C Beginnings Series

Andi's Pony Trouble
Andi's Indian Summer
Andi's Fair Surprise
Andi's Scary School Days
Andi's Lonely Little Foal
Andi's Circle C Christmas

Circle C Beginnings

Andi's Fair Surprise

Susan K. Marlow
Illustrated by Leslie Gammelgaard

Kregel
Publications

Andi's Fair Surprise
©2011 by Susan K. Marlow

Illustrations ©2011 by Leslie Gammelgaard

Published by Kregel Publications, a division of Kregel, Inc., P.O. Box 2607, Grand Rapids, MI 49501.

ISBN 978-0-8254-4184-4

Printed in the United States of America
11 12 13 14 15 / 5 4 3 2 1

Contents

New Words 7

1. Ribbons and Roosters 9
2. All Tied Up 17
3. The Black Beast 23
4. Surprises 29
5. Tickets 35
6. Fair Day 41
7. The Prize 47
8. Winning Ticket 53
9. Lamb Trouble 59
10. Blue Ribbon 65

A Peek into the Past 73

New Words

calf	a baby cow
dull	not exciting; boring
exhibits	the booths at a fair that show animals, crafts, and other fair items
foreman	someone who helps the rancher take care of his ranch
grandstand	the seats at a fair where people can watch big events like a horse race
lasso	a rope with a loop tied at one end
livestock	farm animals
midway	the part of a fair where you find games, food, and thrill shows (and, in our day, rides)
soot	tiny specks of leftover wood or coal after it is burned
thrill show	an exciting event at the fair, like the sword swallower or the strong man

Chapter 1

Ribbons and Roosters

Andi Carter jumped off the back porch and ran across the yard. She was always running . . . or jumping.

Right now she was carrying her very own lasso.

"Here, Duke!" she called.

Andi wound her lasso into big loops and called Duke again. Where *was* that dog?

Just then a big yellow dog ran up, tail wagging. His tongue came out. He licked Andi's face.

Andi wiped her cheek. *Yuck!* Dog kisses.

But she patted Duke on the head and said, "Good dog. Now, sit."

Duke plopped down. His tail thumped the dusty ground.

Andi backed up. She took one step, two steps, three steps . . . all the way to ten steps.

"Hold still, Duke," she told the dog.

Duke cocked his head and whined, but he sat still.

Andi swung the lasso over her head. Then she threw it out as far as she could.

Thunk!

The rope came down in a tangle on Duke's nose. He yelped and dashed away.

"Come back here!" Andi shouted.

Duke kept running.

"How am I ever going to learn to be a cowboy if you don't let me practice roping you?" she yelled at Duke.

Andi kicked the dust. She wished she could lasso a real calf. But her big brother Chad would not let her. He said a calf was too big and too wild for a six-year-old girl to rope.

Roping a horse was Andi's second-best idea. Her pony Coco always stood still when Andi tried to throw a lasso around his neck. She

missed every time. Coco was a little bit too tall.

That left the ranch dogs. But they always ran away when Andi's lasso hit them on the head.

Andi wound her rope into loops again and let out a big breath. "What is left to lasso on this ranch?"

Then she smiled. The chickens!

"Here, chick, chick, chick," Andi called to the hens scratching in the dirt.

She looked around to see if Henry the Eighth was nearby. That mean old rooster would not like it if she lassoed his hens.

For once, Henry was nowhere in sight.

"He's probably waiting to jump out and peck me," Andi said to herself. She did not like that rooster.

Not one teensy bit.

But Henry the Eighth was not waiting to jump out at Andi. He could not jump out and peck anybody. He was sitting in a cage near the chicken coop.

Andi's friend Riley was standing right next to him.

Andi dropped her rope and ran over to Riley.

"What's Henry doing in that cage?" she asked.

"I'm getting him used to it," Riley said. "I'm taking him to the fair next week. I figure he'll win a blue ribbon. He's a beautiful rooster."

"He's a *mean* rooster," Andi said. But her heart started to thump. *A blue ribbon!*

"I want to win one of those ribbons too," she told Riley. "So I'm going to take Taffy to the fair. She's the prettiest foal in all of California. She'll win a blue ribbon for sure."

Riley laughed. "You can't take Taffy to the fair. They don't have contests for baby horses."

"Just because you're eight years old doesn't mean you know everything," Andi huffed. "If you can take Henry to the fair, then I can take Taffy."

Riley shrugged and pointed. "There's Chad. Go ask him and see what he says."

Andi's big brother was heading for the barn. Riley's Uncle Sid—the ranch foreman—was with him. The men were talking and laughing together.

Andi skipped over to her brother. She gave him a big smile.

"Guess what, Chad," she said. "I'm taking Taffy to the fair. She'll win a blue ribbon, on account of she's so pretty . . . and smart."

Chad didn't say anything.

Sid raised his eyebrows and didn't say anything either.

"Riley's taking Henry, so I can take Taffy," Andi explained. "Right?"

Chad shook his head. "Not this year. Taffy's too little, and so are you."

Andi stamped her foot. Dust flew up. "I am *not* too little!"

Everybody was always telling Andi she was too little.

"I'm sorry, but you are not taking Taffy to the fair," Chad said.

"Taffy is my very own horse," she told Chad. "I can take her if I want to. I'm going to get her ready right now."

Andi turned and stomped away. "You are not the boss of me!" she yelled over her shoulder.

Bossy old Chad. He was always spoiling her great ideas.

Andi ran toward the pasture, where Taffy and Coco were eating grass.

Suddenly, Andi felt something tight go around her. She felt a quick jerk.

Then *thud!* She was sitting on the ground. Just like that.

Chapter 2

All Tied Up

Andi gasped. A rope held her arms tight against her sides. She couldn't move. She couldn't get up.

She was tied up tighter than a calf.

"Hold your horses," Chad said. "You're not going anywhere. Not until you settle down."

"No!" Andi wiggled and squirmed. "Let me go!"

Chad pulled the lasso tighter. "Nope."

Riley and Sid walked over. Sid was chuckling.

Riley's eyes were big and full of surprise. He was not laughing. He looked at Andi and didn't say a word.

He probably doesn't want to get lassoed next, Andi thought.

Riley was a little scared of bossy Chad. But Andi wasn't. Not one bit. Chad was always teasing her.

Only, this time he didn't look like he was teasing.

"Are you ready to behave yourself?" Chad asked. "You are *not* taking Taffy to the fair."

Andi scowled at Chad. But she didn't talk back. Not this time. She didn't like being tied up like a calf.

Chad squatted down beside Andi. He loosened the rope and pulled it over her head. Then he handed it to her.

"This is your rope," he said, grinning. "You left it lying on the ground."

Chad ruffled Andi's hair and stood up.

Andi's cheeks grew hot. Tied up with her own lasso! What kind of mean trick was that?

She jumped up and threw her rope on the ground. Then she made her hand into a fist. She swung at Chad.

"You're mean and bossy!" Andi shouted.

"Whoa there," Chad said, catching her arm. "I don't have time for this. I have work to do."

Still grinning, he picked Andi up. He turned

her upside down and held her legs tight. Then he headed for the ranch house.

Andi felt dizzy. Her two braids dragged in the dust. She yelled and swung her arms. She tried to kick.

But no matter what Andi did, she could not wiggle free.

Chad turned her right side up and set her down on the back porch. "Here she is, Mother," he said.

Then Chad walked away.

Andi looked up. She stopped yelling.

Mother stood there, looking down at her. She was not smiling.

Andi gulped.

Mother had not told Chad, *Don't tease your sister*. In fact, it looked like Mother was glad Chad had roped Andi and brought her to the house.

It looked like Mother was on Chad's side.

"Did you see what Chad did?" Andi said, all in a rush. "He lassoed me and told me I can't take Taffy to the fair. Then he—"

"I saw what happened," Mother said. She sat down on the porch swing. Then she pulled Andi onto her lap. "Chad's right. You may not take Taffy to the fair."

Andi's shoulders slumped.

"Justin, Chad, and Mitch are taking lots of cows and horses to the fair," Andi said. "You're taking the jars of jelly you made. Melinda is showing her quilt. And Riley is taking Henry."

She rubbed her eyes. "Everybody will win a blue ribbon. Everybody but me."

Mother hugged Andi. "Not everybody wins a ribbon, sweetheart."

"But Taffy would," Andi said. "I know she would!"

Mother shook her head. "Caring for an animal at the fair is a lot of work. You may take Taffy when you're old enough to do the work yourself. Not this year."

She slid Andi from her lap and stood up. "And you will tell Chad you're sorry for acting up about it."

The talking was over.

"Yes, Mother," Andi whispered.

Mother reached into her sewing basket next to the porch swing.

"Look," she said with a smile. "I'm making you something special to wear to the fair. You'll look cute as a button."

Andi squinted at the dress Mother held up. It was a pretty, blue-and-white dress.

And what was Mother holding in her other

hand? It looked like a straw hat with a wide, blue ribbon.

Uh-oh.

"I have to wear a fancy dress to the fair?" Andi asked.

"Of course," Mother said. "Everybody dresses up for the fair."

She plopped the hat on Andi's head and held the new dress up to Andi's shoulders.

Andi looked down. *Cute as a button?*

"Buttons are not cute," Andi said. "Buttons are dull."

Which is what this fair is beginning to sound like too.

But she didn't say that part out loud.

Chapter 3

The Black Beast

The week went by faster than a galloping horse. Andi wished she were home, playing with Taffy.

Instead, she was in town, waiting for the train. It would take hours and hours to get to the state fair on the train.

Worse, Andi was dressed "cute as a button." But so was her big sister, Melinda. Even Riley wore new clothes, and his hair was combed. For once.

Far away, a train whistle blew.

Soon, Andi saw black smoke puffing up from the train's smokestack. She watched the train pull up next to the platform. She had never been this close to a train before.

Her heart pounded as the black beast rushed toward her.

The whistle blew again.

Andi covered her ears. A train whistle sounded a lot louder up close than it did from far away.

And why did they have to blow that whistle anyway? Everybody could see the train was coming. It was too big to hide.

The black engine screeched to a stop. Steam rolled from the wheels. A bell clanged.

It was time to get on the train.

Riley yanked on Andi's hand. "Come on. I want to see inside."

Andi was not excited about climbing into the belly of that huge black beast. But she was not going to tell Riley that.

She looked up at her mother.

Mother smiled. "Go ahead. You may choose our seats."

Riley let out a big whoop. He dragged Andi up the metal steps and into the passenger car.

Andi's eyes opened wide. "Oh, my!"

The passenger car looked like a fancy room. There were wide, red velvet seats on both sides of a long walkway. Large glass windows let the sunshine in.

Riley plopped down in a seat next to a window.

"I want to sit by a window too," Andi said.

She climbed into the seat in front of Riley. Her oldest brother, Justin, sat down beside her. Then Mother sat down.

Andi smiled. She liked sitting next to Justin. He was always patient. Sitting with Justin felt just as nice as sitting beside Father when he was alive. Being near Justin helped Andi not miss Father so much.

A few minutes later the train whistle blew.

Andi looked out the window. A man in a dark blue uniform was calling, "All aboard!"

Soon there was a roar and a big jerk. Andi fell back against her seat.

Then another jerk threw Andi forward. She bumped her nose on the seat in front of her.

Ouch!

"Let me off this train!" Andi hollered. "I don't want to bounce and slide around all day."

"You'll be fine," Justin told her.

Andi wasn't so sure about that.

The train went faster. It swayed back and forth.

Andi had to hold on to Justin's arm to keep from sliding off the slippery seat. Her straw hat kept falling down in front of her eyes. Her stomach felt sick.

And the train had only been moving for ten minutes.

The day did not get better. The train clacked along the tracks, hour after hour. The sun shone hot and bright through the windows.

Andi stared out the window. She felt stuffy. The sun was shining in her face.

Then she got an idea. *Maybe I can let some air inside.*

Andi reached up and pulled on the latch.

Clunk!

The window came down fast. The hot August wind blew in Andi's face.

And that wasn't all that blew in.

A cloud of tiny black specks flew inside. The specks landed in Andi's lap and all over Mother's new dress.

They blew all over everybody else too.

Andi sneezed.

"Close the window," Mother said in a hurry.

Andi jumped to obey.

But the window was too heavy to push back in place. The black specks kept coming in. People began to complain.

Justin reached over and took care of it.

"Windows on trains are best left closed," he said.

"What are all these black specks?" Andi asked. She sneezed again. "They smell terrible."

"It's soot," Mother said.

Andi looked at Mother's dress. It wasn't yellow anymore. Instead, it looked like a yellow-and-black speckled dress.

Uh-oh, Andi thought. *Soot must be just like dirt. Now there's dirt all over Mother's new dress.*

"Where did all this soot come from?" Andi asked.

Riley popped up from behind Andi's seat.

"The engine burns coal, and that makes the train go," he explained. "The more coal it burns, the faster it goes. The leftover coal goes out the smokestack. That's the sooty stuff."

"Oh!" Andi said, very impressed. Riley sure knew a lot about trains.

The only thing Andi knew about trains was that they made her feel sick. And they took a long, long time to get where they were going.

Andi yawned. *Let me off this train!*

Only this time, she kept her thoughts to herself.

Chapter 4

Surprises

Andi opened one eye. Then she opened her other eye.

It was quiet. No loud train whistle. No *clackety-clack*. No roaring.

Andi sat up and smiled. *Hooray!* She was no longer on the train.

Andi could not remember the rest of that long ride. She must have fallen asleep after supper and slept and slept.

And she woke up . . . where?

Andi looked around. The room was full of sunshine and lace.

There were fancy lace curtains and big glass windows. A sparkly lamp hung from the high ceiling. Rugs covered the floor.

The beds were soft.

Andi did a little bounce.

Very soft.

Melinda was asleep, right next to Andi in the same bed. Across the room, Mother was sleeping in her own bed.

Then Andi remembered. "It's Fair Day!"

All of a sudden, the fair sounded like the most exciting thing in the world.

She shook Melinda. "Wake up, sleepyhead. It's Fair Day."

Melinda rolled over. Her eyes flew open. She giggled. "Fair Day!"

Andi stood up and bounced. *This bed is so bouncy!* She laughed and jumped again.

Melinda yanked on Andi's white nightgown.

"Don't jump on the bed," she whispered. "If you break it, then where will we sleep all week?"

Andi fell on top of Melinda. "All week?"

"The fair lasts a whole week," Melinda said.

She pushed Andi away and climbed out of bed. "You don't think we can see everything in one day, do you?"

Andi didn't answer. She followed Melinda off the bed and began to get dressed.

Melinda kept talking. "There's so much to see at the fair! Animals and needlework and baked goods and fruits and vegetables—and everything else you can think of. There are horse races and thrill shows and a shooting contest."

Melinda sat down and buttoned Andi's new dress up the back.

"Best of all is the last day," she said. "That's when some of the exhibits give away prizes. If your fair ticket has the right number on it, you win something."

Andi twisted around to look at her sister. "Like candy?"

"There are much better prizes than candy," Mother said from across the room. She was already putting on her shoes.

"Better than candy?" Andi asked. What could be better than candy?

Mother smiled. "You'll see. Now hurry up, girls. We don't want to be late for breakfast. We have a lot to do before we can enjoy the fair."

Mother combed Andi's hair into two braids. She tied blue ribbons on the ends of the braids. Then she put the straw hat on Andi's head and opened the door.

Andi looked around. Their fancy room was a big mess.

"Don't we have to clean our room?" she asked.

Melinda giggled. "That's the fun of staying in a hotel, Andi. No chores."

Andi smiled at her sister. This fair was sounding better and better.

Andi got another surprise downstairs.

The whole family, plus Riley and his Uncle Sid, were eating breakfast in the hotel dining room. Mother said Andi could choose anything she wanted from the menu.

Andi's eyes got bigger and bigger when Melinda read the menu to her. So many choices!

She took a big breath. "I want pancakes and bacon and eggs and a dish of peaches and—"

"Slow down," Justin said, laughing. He gave Andi's order to the smiling waitress.

It was the best breakfast Andi ever ate, but Justin had to help her finish it.

"Somebody's eyes were bigger than her stomach," he said when breakfast was over.

Everybody stood up to leave.

"We have to take care of the livestock," Chad said. "Riding in the cattle car yesterday probably didn't do them any good."

"I have to feed Henry and give him some water," Riley said.

"Melinda needs to put her quilt with the others," Mother added. "And I must see to my jars of jelly."

All of a sudden Andi felt grumpy. Everybody had something special to enter in the fair. Everybody would win a blue ribbon.

Everybody but me, Andi thought.

She let out a big sigh and followed her family out of the hotel.

The sun was hot and bright. Andi blinked. Then she remembered something.

"My hat!" she yelled. "I forgot my hat."

Andi turned and dashed back into the hotel. She ran into the dining room.

Her straw hat was sitting on the table, right where she left it.

Only . . . there was a surprise for Andi. Two shiny dimes sat next to her hat.

Andi clapped her hands. Justin had left money for her to spend at the fair!

He's the best brother in the whole world, she thought with a smile.

Andi picked up the money and slipped it into her dress pocket.

Then she raced back to find her family.

Chapter 5

Tickets

It took no time at all to find a buggy and driver to take Andi and her family to the fairgrounds.

Andi rode in the buggy and watched the city of Sacramento go by. She had never seen so many tall buildings. She had never seen so many people.

Sacramento is a little scary, Andi thought.

But not so scary that she was going to tell anybody about it.

When the buggy stopped in front of the fair gate, Andi jumped out. She didn't even wait. She was too excited to see the fair.

"Don't run ahead, Andrea," Mother said. "You must stay with one of us at all times."

"And you can't even go in until you buy a ticket," Riley hollered at her.

Oops!

Andi had forgotten about the ticket. Her ticket might win her a prize on the last day.

She ran up to Justin and tugged on his sleeve. "Make sure I get a winner, Justin."

Melinda giggled. "You can't choose a winning ticket, Andi. They just pick a number. If your ticket matches, then you win."

Justin winked at Andi. Then he held out the tickets he had just bought.

"Andi can choose first," he said, "because she's the littlest."

At last! One good reason for being little.

Actually, the only good reason so far, Andi thought.

She looked at the tickets in Justin's hand. Which one should she pick?

"Just close your eyes and pick one," Riley said.

Andi shook her head. She had to choose the right ticket.

The *winning* ticket.

"Hurry up, Andi," Melinda said.

But Andi took her time.

Then she saw the perfect ticket. It had the number 696 stamped on it.

She picked it up and said, "I'm six years old. This ticket has two sixes and one nine. And nines are just like sixes, almost. Only upside down."

"Good choice, honey," Justin said. He then let Melinda and Riley choose their tickets.

"Would you like me to keep your ticket for you?" Mother asked Andi.

"No, thank you." Andi folded her ticket in half. "I don't want my winning ticket to get mixed up with yours."

Mother smiled. "Then I'll pin it in your pocket so you don't lose it."

When Andi's ticket was safely pinned inside her dress pocket, Justin showed her two shiny dimes.

"Here's twenty cents to spend at the fair today," he said.

Andi's eyes opened wide. "*More* money?" She reached into her other pocket. "You already gave me two dimes." She held them up. "See?"

Justin wrinkled his eyebrows, like he was puzzled. "Where did you get those?"

"In the hotel dining room," Andi said. "You left them on the table next to my hat."

"Oh, dear," Mother said.

Justin let out a long, slow breath.

Nobody else said a word.

Then Chad chuckled, and Mitch grinned.

"That was the tip," Melinda said, giggling.

"And you took it," Riley said. "Boy, are you in trouble!"

Riley's Uncle Sid hushed him up.

"What's a . . . what's a tip?" Andi asked, a little shaky. She looked at the two dimes in her hand. She stole a tip. Would she go to jail?

Mother knelt beside Andi and hugged her.

"A tip is the money we give to the waitress who served our food," she said. "It's an extra thank-you for her work. Justin left it on the table for her to find."

"But you took it instead," Melinda said.

"Melinda," Mother said. That meant, *Be quiet*.

Quick as a wink, Andi gave the tip money back to Justin. She did not want to be a thief—not even by accident.

Her heart thumped.

"I'm sorry," she said. "I thought Justin left me the money for a surprise."

"It's all right," Mother told her. "You didn't know. Here's *your* fair money. We'll wrap it in a hanky and pin it in your other pocket."

Andi's thumpy heart felt better after that.

She patted her two pockets. One pocket held twenty whole cents to spend at the fair. The other pocket held a winning ticket.

She was sure of it!

Chapter 6

Fair Day

Andi did not want to go with Mother and Melinda to enter their things in the fair. Jars of jelly and pretty quilts did not sound very interesting to look at.

"Can I . . . *may* I go with Riley?" Andi asked.

"I'll look after her," Sid told Andi's mother. "She can help Riley with the rooster. Then I'll take them around to see the horses. We can meet up later."

Andi thought this was a good plan. She wanted to see how much work it was to take an animal to the fair.

Mother said yes.

"Come on, Andi!" Riley shouted. He took

off for the chicken exhibits. By the time Andi caught up, he was inside the big building.

Andi stopped short. Inside that building were dozens and dozens of cages. The cages were full of roosters and hens and fluffy chicks.

And what a noise! Clucking and crowing and cackling and cheeping.

"Oh, my!" Andi said. She had never seen so many chickens in one place.

But they were all locked up.

Poor little things, Andi thought.

Then Andi saw Henry, and she was glad he was locked up.

That rooster looked mad about being in a cage. His black eyes glared at Andi. He made a low, scary noise in his throat.

Andi wasn't afraid. Not this time. Henry was locked up good and tight.

"I have to check on Henry every couple of hours," Riley told her. "He has to have lots of water, on account of it's so hot."

"That doesn't sound like much fun," Andi said. It was a long walk across the fairgrounds just to check on a rooster all day long.

"If you think a rooster drinks a lot of water,

you should see how much the horses drink," Sid said with a laugh. "And water buckets are heavy."

"Maybe leaving Taffy on the ranch was a good idea," Andi said quietly, just to herself. It was hot today, and a little foal would need a lot of care.

Riley gave Henry food and water. Then he tapped Andi on the shoulder.

"Let's go see the horses," he said.

So Andi and Riley and Uncle Sid went to the horse barn.

It looked like there were more than a hundred horses in that place! They came in all different sizes and colors. Andi even saw a golden horse the same color as Taffy.

But she did not see any baby horses. Chad was right. Taffy was too little to go to the fair.

Then Uncle Sid took Andi and Riley to see the cattle.

Andi was not excited about cattle.

"I can see cows and bulls on the ranch," she said.

She was not excited about pigs either. They squealed so much that Andi had to cover her ears. And they smelled stinky.

Andi ran out of the hog barn as fast as she could.

The sheep were last.

Uncle Sid almost didn't let Andi go into that barn. He said sheep men and cattlemen didn't get along too well. He didn't want to see any smelly sheep.

But Andi did. Her favorite Bible story was about a little lost sheep. She wanted to see one of those lambs for herself.

"Please?" she begged.

Riley rolled his eyes.

Sid sighed. Then he took Andi and Riley into the large building.

There were a lot of exhibits in the sheep barn. Next to the pens of wooly sheep and frisky lambs, some ladies were spinning wool. Their spinning wheels went around and around, turning the wool into yarn.

"My name is Carrie," a little girl told Andi. "Do you want to pet my sheep?"

"Oh, yes!" Andi climbed into the pen with the girl and her sheep. She sank her fingers into the creamy wool. "It's so soft!"

Carrie smiled. "Her name is Miss Rose."

Riley wrinkled his nose. "She sure doesn't *smell* like a rose."

Andi pretended not to hear Riley.

"Do you have any baby lambs?" she asked.

Carrie's smiley face turned sad. She shook her head. "As soon as they got big enough, Papa sold them."

Carrie pointed to a large pen in the corner of the barn. "But you can see lambs over there."

The pen was full of little lambs and their mamas.

The lambs leaped in the air. They butted each other with their fuzzy heads. They said *baa, baa* over and over.

"*Baa, baa!*" Andi called back to them.

She could not stop giggling. No wonder Jesus loved little lambs. They were so sweet . . . and so funny.

When Andi left the sheep barn, she said, "My first-favorite animal is a horse. But my second-best animal is a lamb."

"Lambs are cute," Riley said. "But they grow up to be smelly sheep."

Sid grunted. That meant he agreed with Riley.

Andi didn't care. She liked lambs.

And she liked the fair.

Chapter 7

The Prize

The fair got better and better. There was so much to do and see, just like Melinda said.

Some of the time, Mother let Andi and Riley see the fair with Melinda. Melinda was eleven years old. She was old enough to look after Andi and Riley.

Sometimes the girls helped Riley take care of Henry the Eighth. Sometimes they stopped at the sheep barn so Andi could play with the lambs.

But most of the time, the whole family did things together.

They ate fried chicken and hot, buttered corn on the cob.

They drank ice-cold lemonade.

They watched the hot air balloon take a basket full of people way up in the sky.

Melinda wanted to ride in the basket too, but Mother said no. It was too dangerous.

Later, they all watched the horses run around the big racetrack. Andi's throat got sore from yelling for her brother to win.

"Faster, Mitch! Faster!" she screamed, jumping up and down in her seat.

A thousand other people stood up in the grandstand and yelled too. But they probably were not yelling for Mitch to win.

Mitch didn't win, but he got a third-place ribbon. Andi thought that was pretty good for a sixteen-year-old boy.

Every day, Justin gave Andi twenty cents to spend on whatever she wanted.

She spent a few pennies on taffy at the candy-making booth. It was still warm when the lady snipped off a chunk of the chewy, golden candy and dropped it in her hand.

Andi spent a nickel to see the thrill show with Melinda. Melinda wanted to see the strong man.

"I don't want to waste a whole nickel just to see a strong man," Andi grumbled.

But Andi had to do what Melinda said. If she didn't, Andi would have to spend the day looking at grown-up exhibits with Mother. Needlework, like bonnets and pillowcases, did not thrill Andi.

It was better to let Melinda be the boss.

So Andi paid her nickel and went inside the big tent with Melinda and Riley.

When the strong man brought out a pony, Andi perked up. She yanked on Melinda's sleeve.

"What's he going to do with that pony?" she asked.

"Wait and see," Melinda said.

The strong man lifted the pony up on his shoulders.

Andi gasped. Shivers went up and down her arms. No wonder Melinda called it a thrill show. Andi felt very thrilled!

She clapped and clapped. "Hooray for the strong man!"

"Hooray, hooray!" Riley and Melinda shouted.

Later that week Andi found something better than a strong man. Better than a horse race. Better even than taffy candy.

It was a game, and it only cost a nickel.

"Look, Melinda!" Andi grabbed her sister's hand and pointed. "What does that sign say?"

"Ring Toss," Melinda told her. "For five

cents you can throw three rings. If one of them lands on a peg, you get to choose a prize."

Andi grinned. Lots of pegs were sticking out of a big wall. How could she miss?

And she knew exactly which prize she wanted to win.

It was a cowboy hat—just like Riley and her brothers wore. Only, it had a big, red feather sticking out of the hatband.

"I want to win that hat," she told Melinda. "The one with the feather."

Melinda shook her head. "This game is harder than it looks. Don't waste your money. You have a nice hat already." She tapped Andi's straw hat.

Andi didn't listen. She had her eye on that prize.

Andi paid her nickel and took the three rings. She threw them all, but she did not catch a peg.

No matter how many times Andi threw those rings, she could not catch a peg.

Pretty soon all the nickels Andi had saved up were gone. The cowboy hat with the red feather still hung from the hook.

But Andi did not give up.

"I'll try again tomorrow," she said. "For sure I'll toss those rings just right tomorrow."

"It will be your last chance," Riley said. "Because tomorrow is the last day of the fair."

Chapter 8

Winning Ticket

The next morning, Justin gave Andi two more dimes.

"This is the last day of the fair," he said. "Have fun."

Riley and Uncle Sid went to check on Henry. Andi's brothers headed for the horse barn.

"Come on, Melinda," Andi said.

She dragged her sister over to the Ring Toss game. "I'm going to win that hat. I have to. Today is the last day."

But Andi did not win the hat, and now her money was gone.

A few tears leaked out. Andi sniffed and rubbed her eyes.

Melinda gently squeezed Andi's hand. "Don't cry, Andi. It's just a hat. Don't you remember what day it is?"

"The *last* day," Andi grumbled.

Melinda pulled out her fair ticket. "It's the day we find out if we have a winning ticket."

A winning ticket!

Andi wiped her tears away in a hurry. Then she dug into her pocket and unpinned her ticket.

She held it up with a smile. "Here it is. Number six-nine-six, the winning ticket."

Melinda grinned. "We'll walk around to all the exhibits and see which numbers they picked. Maybe your ticket will match."

Then Melinda giggled. "Maybe you'll win an ax or a new pair of boots."

"I'm only going to visit the exhibits I like," Andi said. "Like the taffy booth. *Mmmm* . . . yummy." She licked her lips.

But Andi's ticket did not match the numbers at the candy booths. It didn't match any numbers in the big exhibit hall either. Pretty soon, Andi was ready to win even a pair of boots.

She wanted to take *something* home from the fair.

Just then, Riley ran up.

"How is mean old Henry today?" Andi asked.

Riley held up a white ribbon. "He won third place. He might have won a blue ribbon, but he pecked the judge."

Andi laughed.

Riley yanked on Andi's arm. "They're giving away animals in the barns. Let's see if our tickets match. I want to win a pig."

Andi wrinkled her nose. *No pigs for me!*

It looked like there were no pigs for Riley either. His ticket didn't match.

Andi's ticket almost matched the number to win a pony. But she was glad she didn't win. Coco and Taffy were enough work for now.

They went to the sheep barn last.

Andi waved to the little girl named Carrie. Carrie waved back.

"Are they giving away any sheep in here?' Andi asked.

"Just a bum lamb," Carrie told her. She pointed to a corner pen. "He's got no mama, so nobody wants him."

She looked down. "Except me. But my ticket doesn't match."

"Your ticket better not match either, Andi," Melinda said. She sounded like she knew something Andi didn't.

Andi skipped over to the pen. Inside was the cutest black lamb Andi had ever seen. He wasn't very old.

The lamb looked at Andi and said, *Baa, baa!*

Andi's heart pounded. All of a sudden she wanted that lamb. She wanted that lamb more than anything in the whole world.

Even more than the cowboy hat with the red feather.

Andi looked around for the winning number. She found it written above the lamb pen: 696.

Andi gasped. *Her* ticket had 696 stamped on it. She unfolded it to make sure.

"Melinda!" she squealed. "My ticket matches! I win a lamb! A little black lamb!"

Riley's eyes got big. "Really?"

The farmer standing next to the pen took Andi's fair ticket. He looked at it and smiled.

"You're right, missy," he said. "The lamb is all yours."

He reached into the pen and picked up the lamb. Then he set the little animal down at Andi's feet.

Andi dropped to the ground. "Thank you!" She hugged the lamb.

"You'll need this," the farmer said.

Andi looked up.

The farmer was holding a glass bottle with a rubber tip on the end. It was full of milk. He gave it to Andi.

When the lamb saw the bottle, he butted Andi with his fuzzy black head.

Baa, baa! he cried. He looked hungry.

Andi held the bottle and let the lamb suck the milk.

"Oh, Melinda!" she said. "What should I name my new lamb?"

Melinda shook her head. She was not smiling.

"You won't have that lamb long enough to name it," she said.

Andi wrinkled her eyebrows. "Why not?"

"Because cattle ranchers don't like sheep," Melinda said. "Sheep eat the grass all the way down to the dirt. Then the cows don't have anything to eat."

She shrugged. "And we're cattle ranchers."

Riley was nodding. "Remember what Uncle Sid said? He doesn't like smelly sheep."

"Well, *I* like sheep," Andi huffed. "And so does Jesus. I won this lamb, and I'm going to keep him."

"That's what *you* think," Melinda said. "Just wait till Chad sees this lamb."

Chapter 9

Lamb Trouble

Andi let the lamb have two more slurps of milk. Then she pulled the bottle out of his mouth.

Baa, baa! the lamb bleated.

"Do you have a rope I can tie around his neck?" Andi asked the farmer. "I don't want to lose my lamb."

The farmer's eyes twinkled. "No need, missy. Just carry the bottle around. He'll follow you."

Andi stood up and walked a few steps. The lamb ran after her. She ran out of the sheep barn. The lamb followed, bleating.

Riley and Melinda hurried to catch up.

"Where are you taking that lamb?" Melinda wanted to know.

"I'm going to find Mother and show her my

prize," Andi explained. "Now, everybody in the family won something at the fair. You got a blue ribbon for your quilt. Mother got a blue one for her jelly. The boys won prizes too. They got ribbons for the bull and the horses. Even Riley got a ribbon for mean old Henry."

Andi beamed. "And *I* won a lamb."

"You can't take him through the midway," Melinda said. "There are too many people."

"It's the fastest way to find Mother," Andi said. She patted her lamb and showed him the bottle. "He'll follow me."

The midway was crowded with people.

Ladies with long, wide skirts swished by Andi. Children ran past. People selling food and trinkets called out.

The lamb followed Andi through the crowd.

Whenever he fell behind, Andi shook the bottle of milk and called him. The lamb always skipped back to Andi, bleating. Then she gave him a little drink.

Suddenly, a group of children ran between Andi and her lamb.

The lamb disappeared.

Andi heard his *baa, baa*, but she couldn't see

him. She heard people yelling. Then she heard a crash and more bleating.

Andi, Riley, and Melinda ran toward the crashing and shouting.

Baa, baa! The little black lamb squeezed out from under a tipped-over cart. He ran around in circles. He looked scared.

Two men tried to catch him. The lamb darted the other way. The men tripped and knocked over another cart.

"Oh, no!" Melinda said. She groaned.

Andi heard laughing. Then angry voices began to shout. More people crowded around to watch.

"Don't hurt my lamb!" Andi yelled. She ran toward the lamb, shaking the bottle.

The lamb stopped when he saw the bottle. He ran back to Andi and butted her—hard.

Thud!

Andi fell on the ground. She threw her arms around the lamb's neck and hugged him tight.

Then she gave him a drink of milk.

"I told you not to go through the midway," Melinda scolded. She stood over Andi, with her hands on her hips. "Look at the mess that lamb made!"

Andi looked around. Tipped-over carts and food were everywhere.

How could one little lamb make such a big mess?

Riley started chanting, "Andi had a little lamb. Its fleece was black as ink. And every place that lamb did go, it caused a great big stink."

He laughed.

"That's not funny, Riley," Melinda grouched.

Andi giggled. "I think it's funny. And I just thought of a name for my lamb. Inky."

Melinda reached down and picked up the lamb. It took both arms to hold him.

"Get up, Andi," she said. "I'll carry the lamb. Let's go before something worse happens."

But something worse happened just then.

A man came up and asked, "Is this your lamb, miss?"

Andi and Melinda looked at each other.

Melinda's face turned red. "Yes, sir."

"You need to pay for the mess that little fellow made," the man said. "Broken glass, spoiled food. It has to be paid for."

Andi gulped. *Uh-oh!*

Melinda's face turned even redder. "I . . . I have to find my mother," she said.

But there was no need to find their mother.

"Look," Riley said. "Here come Uncle Sid and Chad."

He waved at them and yelled, "Come see what Andi won!"

Chapter 10

Blue Ribbon

It didn't take Chad long to find out what happened. The man who wanted the money did all of the talking.

Nobody else said a word.

Then Chad pulled out some money and paid the man. The man smiled, shook Chad's hand, and left in a hurry.

Andi was glad about that.

But she didn't stay happy for long.

Chad was frowning. "Where did this animal come from?" he asked.

"I won him," Andi explained. "His name is Inky. He drinks from a bottle."

"You can't keep him," Chad said.

"I can too!" Andi said. "I won him with my

fair ticket. He's my very own lamb. I'm taking him home."

Chad crossed his arms. "No, you're not," he said. "No sheep will ever set foot on the Circle C ranch. Now, take that lamb right back where you got it."

"One little lamb is not a flock of sheep, Chad," Melinda said. "I kind of like him."

Andi smiled. *Hooray for a big sister!* Melinda was on her side.

It was no use. Chad would not give in.

Bossy old Chad.

"You are *not* the boss!" Andi told him. "Mother is the boss. She'll let me take Inky home."

But when they found Mother, Andi got a bad surprise. Mother was the boss of Andi, but she let Chad boss the ranch.

Andi felt sick inside when she heard that.

Then Mother pulled Andi into a tight hug. She pulled Inky into a hug too.

"Look at this little lamb, Andrea," Mother said. "If we take him back to the ranch, he would be the only sheep. He would have no friends."

"I'm his friend," Andi said. "Coco would be his friend too. And Taffy."

"But Inky needs *sheep* friends," Mother said. "Sheep like to be with other sheep."

Andi rubbed her eyes. They were starting to sting.

Mother kept talking. "Remember your favorite Bible story? The one about the lost sheep?"

Andi nodded.

"Why did Jesus go looking for that sheep?" Mother asked.

"Because it was lost," Andi said. "And all alone."

Mother smiled. "That's right, sweetheart. And Jesus brought that lost sheep back."

Andi sniffed and looked at her lamb.

"Inky would be unhappy without other sheep," Mother said. "He would feel just like that lost sheep—all alone. Do you think you could be like Jesus and take Inky back to his sheep friends?"

Andi thought and thought. She thought about how fun it would be to have a lamb. Then she thought about how lonely Inky might be.

Inky didn't belong on a cattle ranch. He belonged with other sheep.

Just then Andi thought of a home for Inky.

"There's a little girl in the sheep barn who would take good care of Inky," she told Mother. "She has sheep, but she wants a lamb. I think Inky would like her."

Mother lifted Inky in her arms and stood up. "Why don't you and I surprise that little girl right now?"

Andi blinked, and a tear leaked out. "You mean . . . right this very minute?"

Mother nodded. "I think that would be best."

A big lump was getting stuck in Andi's throat, but she said, "All right, Mother."

It would be hard to give Inky away. Andi tried to be brave and not cry.

It was even harder not to cry when she gave the lamb to Carrie.

"His name's Inky," Andi said softly.

A few more tears leaked out when she handed Carrie the bottle.

"Thank you, thank you!" Carrie said with a big smile. She hugged Andi. She hugged Inky.

Baa, baa! Inky butted Carrie.

The happy look on Carrie's face did not make Andi feel better. Inky was gone—for good.

Now Andi was the only one who had nothing to take home from the fair. She held Mother's hand and tried not to think about that.

When Andi and Mother got back, Melinda and Chad were whispering to each other.

"Come on, Andi," Chad said. "We've got a prize to win."

Andi wrinkled her eyebrows. "What prize?"

Chad lifted her up and winked. "You'll see."

One minute later, Chad set Andi down on the counter of the Ring Toss game. Then he paid his nickel.

"Watch this," he said.

So Andi watched.

Chad threw one ring—only one. He didn't even need the other two rings. The first ring flew through the air and landed around a big peg.

Just like that.

Andi squealed and clapped her hands.

Hooray for a big brother!

Even a bossy one.

Chad yanked off Andi's straw hat. Then he plopped the cowboy hat with the red feather on her head.

"I heard you had your eye on this hat," he said.

The cowboy hat was a little too big.

Andi didn't care. She pushed the hat up and said, "Thank you, Chad!"

Then she hugged him.

→ ←

It was very late. The sun was sinking low in the sky. The fair was over.

Andi held Melinda's hand and walked slowly out of the fairgrounds. She was so sleepy!

She yawned.

Andi's new hat fell over her eyes. She pushed it out of the way. Then she reached up to touch the big red feather.

She smiled. It had been a good day.

And then the day got even better.

Mother bent down and showed Andi a ribbon. It was the blue ribbon from Mother's special jelly.

"This is for you, Andrea," Mother said. "You win a blue ribbon for giving up your lamb. That was a hard, brave thing to do."

Before Andi could say a word, Mother pinned it on her dress. "Now you have a blue ribbon *and* a prize from the fair. What do you think of that?"

Andi gave Mother a big hug and said, "I think this was the best fair ever!"

A Peek into the Past

Have you ever been to the fair? The California State Fair began in 1854. That's a long time ago! The farmers and ranchers wanted to get together to exhibit their farm crops and their livestock. Everybody had such a good time that they decided to do it again the next year—and the year after that. When the railroad was completed, people from all over California began to go to the fair, just like Andi.

The fair grew. They built a grandstand so people could watch the horse races. They gave prizes for the best horses, cows, sheep, goats, pigs, and chickens. Grown-ups and children made all kinds of craft items to enter in the fair. They won prizes too. Almost anything you can think of could be seen at the fair—like biscuits and pianos, axes, soap, beehives, and even lumps of coal!

There were no rides during the fairs of the 1800s. Rides came much later. Instead, fairgoers liked to see thrill shows—like the strong man, the sword swallower, or even a two-headed calf. There were magic shows and games to play. There were all kinds of new foods to try too.

People looked forward to the fair all year long.

Susan K. Marlow, like Andi, has an imagination that never stops! She enjoys teaching writing workshops, sharing what she's learned as a homeschooling mom, and relaxing on her 14-acre homestead in the great state of Washington.

Leslie Gammelgaard, blessed by the tall trees and flower gardens that surround her home in Washington state, finds inspiration for her artwork in the antics of her lively little granddaughter.

Grow Up with Andi!

Don't miss any of Andi's adventures in the Circle C Beginnings series

Andi's Pony Trouble
Andi's Indian Summer
Andi's Fair Surprise
Andi's Scary School Days
Andi's Lonely Little Foal
Andi's Circle C Christmas

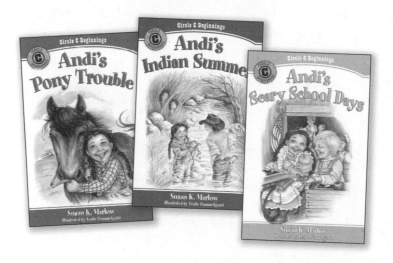

And you can visit www.AndiandTaffy.com
for free coloring pages, learning activities,
puzzles you can do online, and more!

For readers ages 9-14!

Andi's adventures continue in the Circle C Adventures series

Andrea Carter and the Long Ride Home
Andrea Carter and the Dangerous Decision
Andrea Carter and the Family Secret
Andrea Carter and the San Francisco Smugglers
Andrea Carter and the Trouble with Treasure
Andrea Carter and the Price of Truth

Check out Andi's Web site at
www.CircleCAdventures.com